Brontosaurus

Gigantasaurus

Triceratops

Archaeopteryx

Velociraptor

Ankylosaurus

Stegosaurus

Amargasaurus

Brontosaurus

Gigantasaurus

Triceratops

Archaeopteryx

Velociraptor

Ankylosaurus

Stegosaurus

Amargasaurus

For Anthony, who likes to roar!

G.P.

To Chloë and Polly, thank you for being Roarsome!

T.B.

SIMON & SCHUSTER
First published in Great Britain in 2022 by Simon & Schuster UK Ltd
1st Floor, 222 Gray's Inn Road, London, WC1X 8HB
Text copyright © 2022 Gareth Peter • Illustrations copyright © 2022 Tim Budgen
The right of Gareth Peter and Tim Budgen to be identified as the author and illustrator
of this work has been asserted by them in accordance with the Copyright,
Designs and Patents Act, 1988 • All rights reserved, including
the right of reproduction in whole or in part in any form
A CIP catalogue record for this book is available
from the British Library upon request
ISBNs: 978-1-4711-9942-4 (PB) 978-1-4711-9941-7 (eB)
Printed in China
1 3 5 7 9 10 8 6 4 2

WHO WILL YOU MEET ON DINOSAUR STREET?

GARETH PETER • TIM BUDGEN

SIMON & SCHUSTER
London   New York   Sydney   Toronto   New Delhi

What is that stomping and stamping of feet?
It looks like a party on Dinosaur Street.

They're all in a frenzy and eager to go
to the Fizz-whizzing-flash-tastic Fireworks Show!!

HARD ROCK
HARDWARE

Let's give a roar to . . .

Stinkysaurus.

Pinkysaurus.

Teeny-weeny Dinkysaurus.

Bumpysaurus.

Jumpysaurus.

Leave-me-I'm-a Grumpysaurus.

Flashysaurus.

Splashysaurus.

Whoops-there's-been-a Crashysaurus.

Baddiesaurus.

Daddysaurus.

Feeling-lost-and Saddysaurus.

Bikingsaurus.

Hikingsaurus.

Stripes-are-very Strikingsaurus.

Longysaurus.

Strongysaurus.

Surely-this-way's Wrongysaurus.

Actorsaurus.

Tractorsaurus.

Has-the-Dino Factorsaurus.

Slurpysaurus.

Chirpysaurus.

CHIRP CHIRP!

Cheeky-chappy Burpysaurus.

BURP!

Bearysaurus.

Warysaurus.

Yes-we're-nearly There-y-saurus.

We're just in time to watch the show.
Let's gaze into the night . . .

With OOOs and AHHHHs beneath the stars –
it's such a roarsome sight!

Now all the dino-gang is here,
there's one more friend to meet . . .

Let's give a wave to . . . .

...YouASAURUS.

Welcome to our street!

Megalosaurus

Pterodactyl

Allosaurus

Parasaurolophus

Tyrannosaurus Rex

Sinosauropteryx

Iguanodon

Spinosaurus

Diplodocus

Megalosaurus

Pterodactyl

Allosaurus

Parasaurolophus

Tyrannosaurus Rex

Sinosauropteryx

Iguanodon

Spinosaurus

Diplodocus

Brontosaurus

Gigantasaurus

Triceratops

Archaeopteryx

Velociraptor

Ankylosaurus

Stegosaurus

Amargasaurus

Brontosaurus

Gigantasaurus

Triceratops

Archaeopteryx

Velociraptor

Ankylosaurus

Stegosaurus

Amargasaurus

Look out for more hilarious books in the
Who Will You Meet? series!
(And did you spot the ghost character in THIS book?!)

Who Will You Meet on Halloween Street?

coming soon . . .